Quentin Blake

FANTASTIC DAISY ARTICHOKE

RED FOX

for Bousfield School in South Kensington
and for l'Ecole Publique de Chaillevette

Here's our friend Daisy Artichoke

We remember…

...the first day
that we spoke

Her three fat cats
we liked to stroke

Her raven with its
awful croak

Her pig that almost
never woke

Her bike that
almost always broke

Look out!

The pond in which
she liked to soak

Her lovely ragged
patchwork cloak

Her armchair
made of solid oak

The iron stove
she liked to stoke...

...that filled the room
with clouds of smoke.

Amazing Daisy Artichoke!

We love it when she tells a joke

She isn't quite
like other folk –

FANTASTIC...

...DAISY...

...ARTICHOKE!

A Red Fox Book

Published by Random House Children's Books
20 Vauxhall Bridge Road, London SW1V 2SA

A division of The Random House Group Ltd
London Melbourne Sydney Auckland
Johannesburg and agencies throughout the world

3 5 7 9 10 8 6 4 2

First published in the United Kingdom by Jonathan Cape Ltd 1999

Red Fox edition 2001

Printed in Singapore

THE RANDOM HOUSE GROUP Limited Reg. No. 954009

www.randomhouse.co.uk

ISBN 0 09 940006 5